This well-known fairytale is delightfully illustrated and simply retold to entertain all young listeners.

*Titles in Series S852*
**Cinderella**
**Three Little Pigs**
**Goldilocks and the Three Bears**
**Jack and the beanstalk**
**Snow White and the Seven Dwarfs**
These titles are also available as a Gift Box set

British Library Cataloguing in Publication Data
Murdock, Hy
   Cinderella.—(Fairy tales. Series 852; 1)
   I. Title     II. Grundy, Lynn N.     III. Series
   823'.914[J]    PZ8
   ISBN 0-7214-9526-5

First Edition

# Cinderella

written by HY MURDOCK
illustrated by LYNN N GRUNDY

Ladybird Books  Loughborough

Once upon a time there was a beautiful girl called Cinderella. She was good and kind and gentle. But also living in the same house was her cruel stepmother. She had two daughters and they were very ugly.

All of them were very unkind to Cinderella. They wore fine new clothes while Cinderella dressed in rags. And all day long, the ugly sisters made Cinderella wash and cook and clean the house.

One day a messenger came. The prince
was giving a ball and all the ladies
in the land were invited. The two ugly
sisters were going to the ball but
not poor Cinderella because
she didn't have a new
dress to wear.

On the day of the ball, Cinderella had to rush up and down the stairs helping the sisters to get ready. They shouted and argued all day long and Cinderella was pleased when they had gone. But later she wished that she could have gone too, and she began to cry.

Now Cinderella *did* have one good friend. It was her fairy godmother. As the girl sat crying, this kind old lady suddenly appeared and said, 'Cinderella, you can go to the ball!'

They went outside into the garden. The fairy godmother asked Cinderella to find a large pumpkin, six white mice, one rat and four lizards. Then she began to wave her magic wand...

The pumpkin turned into a wonderful golden coach. The mice became six fine white horses. The rat was a coachman,

ready to drive the coach, and the
lizards had turned into four footmen
who would walk beside the coach.

Then the fairy godmother touched Cinderella with her wand. The girl's ragged clothes changed into the most beautiful dress and on her feet were pretty glass slippers.

'Remember one thing,' said her fairy godmother. 'You must be home by midnight. That is when my magic ends.'

So Cinderella went to the ball.

Everyone at the ball thought that
Cinderella was a princess. The prince
danced with her all night, until the clock
began to strike...

**one, two, three, four, five, six**...
Cinderella ran from the ballroom...
**seven, eight, nine, ten, eleven**...

**TWELVE**! As the clock struck midnight, Cinderella was wearing her rags again. She ran away. The prince had tried to follow her but all he could find was one of her glass slippers.

Next day, the prince visited every house to try and find the girl whose foot would fit the slipper. After the ugly sisters had tried, the prince saw Cinderella and asked her to try the glass slipper. This time it *did* fit.

At that moment, Cinderella's fairy godmother appeared again and changed her back into a princess.

The prince asked Cinderella to marry him. They had the most wonderful wedding and everyone was invited — even the ugly sisters. After that, Cinderella and her prince lived happily ever after.